The Travel Adventures of PJ Mouse

• in Canada •

GWYNETH JANE PAGE

Illustrated by Megan Elizabeth

This book is dedicated to my children, Rebecca, Megan, Peter and Emily, for all the wonderful times we have had travelling with PJ. With love from Mom.

I would like to thank Robert Wiersema for helping me get started and for his enthusiastic response to the character of PJ. To Ashley Patton, my gratitude for educating me in how to navigate my way around the computer. And to all my family and friends for their support and encouragement as I learned how to write and become a self published author.

The world according to *PJ*

CANADA

NORTH AMERICA

PACIFIC
OCEAN

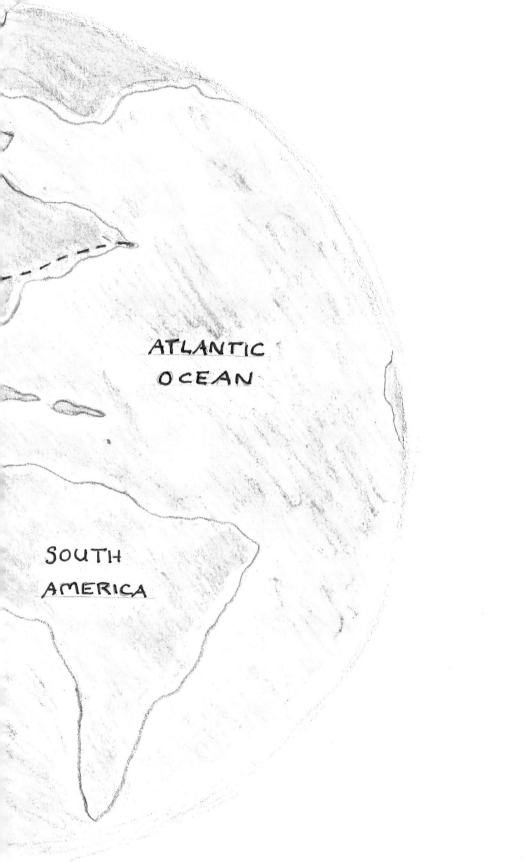

Produced by:

FriesenPress

Suite 300 – 852 Fort Street
Victoria, BC, Canada V8W 1H8

www.friesenpress.com

Distributed to the trade by The Ingram Book Company

Table Of cOntents

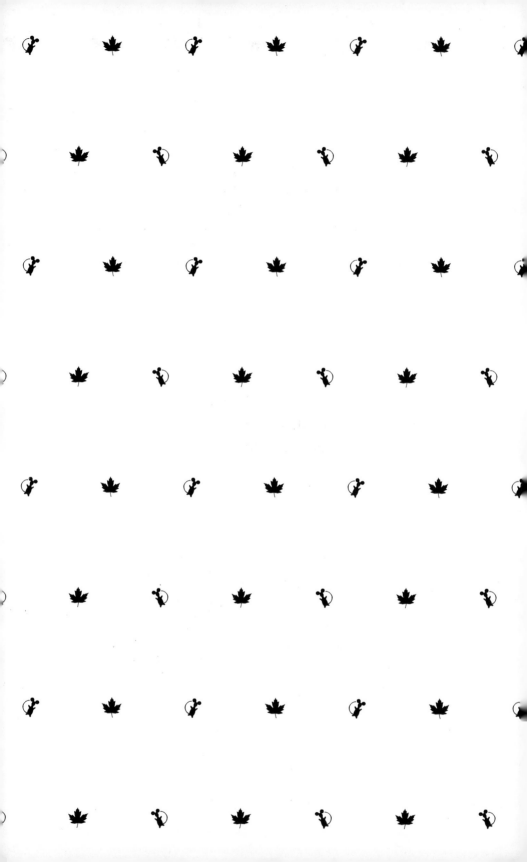

chapter One

IN WHICH PJ FALLS OUT OF A BAG AND INTO A PUDDLE

THUMP. PJ fell from the bag, hit the ground with an "Ouch," rolled for a bit, and ended up in a puddle with an "Oh dear me, what happened?"

PJ looked around and sighed in despair. Nothing but puddles!

Oh dear, oh my, I think I have been lost, thought PJ. *And just when I was so happy to finally be going home from the store. It really was quite comfy riding in the little girl's bag.*

It doesn't look like she is coming back, PJ thought as he watched her feet disappear into the distance. *Oh dear, dear me. Whatever am I to do?*

"Oh help, please help!" PJ cried, but no one seemed to hear.

Oh fiddlesticks, I do believe it is going to rain some more. PJ lay dismally under the bench getting very, very wet.

He watched all the feet rush home out of the storm, wishing that he was going home out of the storm too. He was truly getting quite saturated. "HELP, oh help! Please, can anyone hear me?"

A couple pairs of feet came to a stop in front of the bench.

"Did you hear a noise Mommy?" asked the smaller pair of feet.

"No sweetheart, why?" replied the bigger pair of feet.

"I thought I heard someone yell for help."

Then a face appeared just above the feet. "Oh, look Mommy! There is a little stuffed animal under this bench. He's all wet and dirty, but can I keep him, *please?*"

"Let's take a look," the bigger pair of feet said to the little pair of feet, and with that PJ found himself lifted up by his tail and stared at by some pretty blue eyes. "I think it might be a little mouse. Could be cute when he's all cleaned up. We'll take him home, put him through the wash, and he'll be good as new. Come on now Emily, it's pouring. Let's get home."

Oh, thank goodness, I've been found. Hooray! thought PJ. "Hello, my name is PJ, is your name Emily?" said PJ to the girl who belonged to the small pair of feet.

"Oh, you can talk!" said Emily in a startled voice. "Yes, I'm Emily and this is my mom. But most people seem to call her Jane, so I think that must be her name. Was that you I heard yelling for help?"

"It must have been. You see, I fell out of a bag and

ended up under that bench. Nobody else noticed me, even though I was yelling for help as loudly as a small mouse possibly can. I am very happy you stopped because I was getting awfully wet and feeling quite miserable, all alone in that puddle."

"You *are* quite wet and grubby, but you look like you'll be quite cute when my mom has washed and dried you."

"Oh yes, I am very cute normally."

"I don't think you are supposed to say that about yourself. It sounds conceited."

"What's con…., con…., c….., what you said, mean?" asked PJ.

"I think it's when you think too much of yourself," Emily replied. "At least that's what my sister Rebecca told me it meant when I asked her. It must be true because she knows about lots of things."

"Oh, no, no. I know I am just a very small mouse. It's just that was what was advertised about me at the store. They said I was an 'amazingly cute little mouse.' That's what the salespeople always said to customers. I only thought that they were right about me being very little."

"Yes, well, you are very little. But you are also very cute," Emily told him

"Why thank you very much," said PJ, feeling much more cheerful.

"I'm so happy I found you! This is the best day ever! You can come home with me, and Mommy will wash you up, and then you can live with me and we can have exciting adventures together. Do you like adventures?" Emily asked.

"Well, I don't know. I don't think I have ever had one. Unless you consider getting lost under the bench and ending up in that puddle an adventure. And really, I must admit, I didn't like that too much," PJ told her.

"Funny little mouse. Don't worry, I'll look after you and we'll have lots of fun."

chapter TwO

IN WHICH PJ WALKS ON A GLACIER

PJ felt much, much better. He had been spun round and round, and then head over heels, over head over heels, over heels over head, as he was washed and dried.

He had felt a little dizzy when he was taken out of the dryer, but now that he was so fresh and clean, he didn't really mind being a bit spinny.

"So when are we going on an adventure?" asked PJ of Emily. "Or was that it?"

"No, no. That was just your bath."

"Well, it was quite exciting as far as baths go."

"Yes, I suppose it must have been. Certainly not like any bath that I have ever had. I think our big adventure will begin on Monday. Mom and Dad bought a fifth-wheel for us to travel in," Emily told him.

"What is a fifth-wheel? Is that the wheel you get after your fourth wheel?"

"Silly little mouse. You do say the funniest things. It's kind of like a house on wheels. Want to go and see? It's just out front."

PJ and Emily set off to explore the fifth-wheel.

"I don't see five wheels. In fact I think it has more than that, hmmm, or is it less than that? Either way, I don't think I can count that high. But maybe the people who made it couldn't count that high either and just stopped when they got to five."

"Well, I suppose you could be right."

"It's awfully big," said PJ. "But then I am a very small mouse so most things seem quite large to me."

"Come on. I'll show you around. Look, it's got a kitchen with a fridge and stove and everything, and a bathroom with a shower, and up front here is a bedroom, and back here is a bedroom with bunk beds," Emily said in awe. "Don't you think they look kind of like a big play fort?"

"They do look like a sensible spot to play," said PJ pragmatically.

"I hope I get one of the bunk beds!" said Emily, hopping up and down in excitement.

"Pardon me for being sensible, as it is quite out of character for me, but it does seem that just maybe—although

I could be mistaken—but that the one bed up front and these bunk beds here are not quite enough to sleep all six of you," PJ said curiously.

"Oh. Yes, you are quite correct. But I haven't finished showing you everything yet. See, this table can turn into a bed and the couch turns into another bed. So there's lots of room for all six of us. And you can sleep on my pillow in one of the bunks."

"Yes, well, I suppose I could. But where are we going?" asked PJ.

"My mom said we are going to go see the Rocky Mountains to walk on a glacier."

"What is a glacier?"

"I think it is a really big piece of really old ice."

"Oh," said PJ, thinking that that did not sound too

interesting and certainly not at all like an adventure.

A few days later they all climbed into the big truck that pulled the house on wheels—how many wheels PJ was still not entirely sure—and set off on their first adventure.

"I feel all tingly inside," said PJ.

"That's just the perfect way to describe how I feel too," replied Emily. "This is going to be ever so much fun!"

PJ and Emily stood on the deck of the Spirit of British Columbia, a massive BC Ferry, that was taking them away from their hometown of Victoria. They waved good-bye to Vancouver Island as they watched it fade into the distance, feeling both sad and excited at the same time.

Once they reached the mainland and started driving toward the Rocky Mountains, excitement took over. The scenery they were passing was amazing.

"Look at that lake PJ!" Emily exclaimed. "It's just the same colour as the turquoise crayon I have. Oh, I wish I had brought those crayons with me. Then I could have made a picture of what it looked like."

"And look at those mountains. They look very big. At least they do to a small mouse like me," PJ said.

"Those are the Rocky Mountains. They run for three thousand miles, or four thousand eight hundred kilometers, between Canada and the U. S.. Some of the mountains are over fourteen thousand feet high, or four thousand four hundred meters for those of you who only speak metric," said Emily's sister, Rebecca.

"What is that on the tops of them?" PJ asked.

"I think it must be snow," Emily replied.

"But it's summertime," said PJ in a puzzled sort of way. "I thought we only get snow in the winter when it's very cold out."

"Snow stays in places that are very, very high up because it stays really, really cold up high," replied Rebecca.

"Well, I'm glad we're not up too high then because I don't like being really, really cold! Only a little cold, sometimes, is okay," PJ said with relief.

A while later, Emily's dad announced that they had arrived at the Athabasca Glacier. They all climbed out of the truck to look at the massive sheet of ice that went off into the distance as far as they could see.

"Hold onto the ropes along the trail. I don't want anyone falling down a crevasse," said Emily's mom as they began their trek across the glacier.

"What's a crevasse?" asked Emily.

"A crevasse is a big crack in the ice," replied Rebecca.

PJ, looking down, could see huge cracks in the ice. "Look Emily, the ice is all pretty and blue underneath."

Emily looked, tripped, and PJ went hurtling from his perch on her shoulder in an impressive series of somersaults.

He fell into a crevasse and descended into the icy blue depths of the glacier. *Oh dear, dear me*, thought PJ as he bounced off

        one icy blue ledge,

                cart-wheeled,

          and banged

       into the next.

"Oh, I do hope I stop soon,"

If only I weren't

      so very small

   I might be able

       to get stuck

          and stop

F
a
l
L
i
n
G.

"OUCH!" said PJ, as he bumped into yet another icy shelf, before finally coming to rest on a ledge.

"DADDY!" yelled Emily as she burst into tears.

PJ, looking up from his jewel-like platform, could see all his family looking down at him.

"Oh dear, dear me," moaned PJ. *How will they ever get me out of here?* he thought. *Oh I do always seem to be getting in such a muddle. If only I weren't so very small I wouldn't get into places such as this.*

"B
r
r
r
r
r
r
r!"

PJ started to shiver. *It seems to be cold down low in the ground as well as up high on the mountains. I am glad that normally I just live in the middle.*

And so PJ sat on his shelf, getting quite chilly, as his family up above planned a rescue.

Emily's other sister, Megan, was saying, "Poor little mouse. Whatever are we to do?"

"Is there anything in the first aid kit we could use?" asked Dad.

"There's some tape. We could attach some to your belt and lower it down and try and stick him to it," said Emily's brother, Peter, helpfully.

"Well, it's worth a try," Dad replied.

"Hang on PJ! We have a plan. When you see the tape, stick yourself to it," Emily yelled down to PJ.

"Oh, please do hurry. It is very, very cold down here and I am not particularly fond of being very, very cold," PJ called up to her.

Then PJ saw the belt with a long length of tape attached to it. Once it reached his perch he rolled onto the tape and wrapped it round himself. Amazingly, he felt himself being pulled up between the glistening blue walls of the glacier.

"Oh, thank goodness you are okay and we managed to get you out," said Emily as she gave PJ a big hug, or as big a hug as you can give to a very small mouse.

"I seem to be all in one piece and still have all my stuffing. I suppose I will have to be washed and dried again now, won't I?" he asked her.

"You are a bit grubby," she admitted.

"Oh well, at least that will warm me up!"

"Funny little mouse," Emily smiled.

PJ, now that he was safe, thought that maybe it hadn't been such a bad adventure after all. *Really it was very, very pretty in the crevasse. Much nicer than all this grey ice* on the surface of the glacier. *I really think I quite like the glistening blue depths,* thought PJ; *it's just too bad it is so terribly cold down there.*

Chapter Three

IN WHICH PJ LEARNS TO FLOAT

Emily's family left the mountains behind and ventured into the endless flat prairies in the middle of Canada.

"Why did we stop here Dad?" asked Megan. "I mean, I see the lake and all, but really it's not what I would call a thing of great beauty, or even a very small amount of beauty for that matter."

"No it is definitely not a thing of great beauty. It's a salt water lake. I thought we could all go for a swim to cool off," Dad told her.

"How on earth did a salt water lake come to be here?" asked Peter.

"Well, Saskatchewan is just flat prairie land in the middle of the country now, but apparently it use to be the bottom of the sea many moons ago," Rebecca replied. "The salt content of this lake, called Little Manitou, is five times as much as the ocean. And it is one of only five salt water lakes in the whole world."

"Wow, that's so cool!" said Peter. "I'm all for a swim; it's soooooo hot out. Come on Emily, let's go!"

"As long as Mommy gets my armbands. I am not too good at swimming yet and neither is PJ."

"Well, we have a surprise for you with this lake. I think you and PJ will be just fine," said Mom.

Hmmm, thought PJ as the family headed off to put on their swimsuits, *I wonder what the surprise is. I like surprises. At least, I do most of the time. A swim will be nice; it really is very hot here. I could have done with a bit of this heat when I was stuck in the glacier the other day!*

They all donned their bathing suits and headed for the water. The lake was wonderfully refreshing, sort of, although the water seemed a bit thick or something.

PJ dipped his head into the cool water and popped back up. *Ah, that felt so good,* he thought as he ducked under again, and popped back up. *I really wanted to keep my ears under longer, the coolness feels so good,* so he dipped again and popped right back up. *Hmmm, funny, I don't seem to be able to stay under. This has never been a problem before. Well, maybe I will try floating on my back,* he thought, as he rolled over.

"I feel like I am floating on the very top of the water," said Emily. "And you look like you are, too."

"Me too!" said Peter.

"And look at us!" said Rebecca and Megan as their heads kept popping up from the water.

"We feel like gophers popping out of the ground. We don't seem to be able to stay under the water no matter how hard we try."

"That's the surprise, it's the salt. It makes you float," said Mom.

"Oh," said PJ, not quite understanding why salt would make you float. "But it doesn't help anything float back home. It doesn't matter how much salt I put on my food, it always just stays on the plate. They must have a different kind of salt here in Sask…Sask… in this lake."

"Can we take some of the salt home Mommy to make things float there?"

"No, sweetheart, it doesn't work like that. You will just have to enjoy it while you are here."

"Oh, that's too bad. It would have been fun to show

my friends," said Emily, as she and PJ imagined putting salt on all their food and watching it float away to the amazement of their friends.

And so they all carried on dipping down and popping up until it was time to climb back in the fifth-wheel and head off on their next adventure.

Chapter Four

IN WHICH PJ VISITS NIAGARA FALLS

They drove a long, long way in the fifth-wheel, all the way across the Canadian prairies to the eastern side of the country. They saw fields of wheat, corn, and yellow canola flowers. It was very pretty, but sometimes seemed quite endless. PJ had no idea that Canada was that big. Emily said it even seemed big to her, and she was not a small mouse like him.

Now they were going to see some famous waterfalls. *At least waterfalls will be a nice change from fields of wheat,* thought PJ. He was getting a little weary of looking at the endless flat landscape.

"Come on PJ, time to stretch our legs and go see Niagara Falls," said Emily.

"Oh, can we really stretch my legs? It might make me a bit taller!" PJ asked, excitedly.

"Silly mouse. No, it means take a walk. Stretch your legs is just an expression," said Rebecca.

"Oh, that's too bad. I could do with being just a bit taller."

"You are a funny little mouse. And you are just fine just the way you are," Emily told him.

"Is it starting to rain?" asked Peter.

"No. I think that is the spray from the Falls," said Rebecca.

"Well, it seems like rain. I'm getting very wet," Peter replied.

"Oh look. There they are. WOW, that is a lot of water! And it's SO loud," said Emily.

"It's no wonder it's loud, did you know that these three falls combined, that make up the Niagara Falls, put out the most water of any waterfalls on earth? With that kind of force, it means that the erosion should eradicate the falls in about fifty thousand years!" said Rebecca.

"Well, at least we still have a little bit of time to look at them," replied Megan, sarcastically.

"WHAT?" yelled Emily.

"Did you say something Rebecca? I can't hear you," said PJ.

"It's sooooo LOUD!" said Peter.

"Come on you guys, Mom and Dad are taking us on the boat ride into the Falls," said Rebecca.

Oh, I don't think I like the sound of that, thought PJ. *Why would anyone want to go INTO the falls? That is a lot of water that would be coming down on you. I wonder if maybe they could just leave me here. Oh dear. Guess not.* "I think we are about to get very, very wet," he said out loud.

"I think you might be right PJ," said Peter. "The Falls seem even bigger from down here. And the roar of the water is soooo loud!"

"PARDON? I can't hear you. The water is so loud!" said PJ.

"WHAT did you say? I can't hear you. The roar of the water is so loud!" Peter yelled.

"I said PARDON? I can't hear you. The water is soooo loud!" PJ yelled back.

"I said…oh never mind! Look, I think Emily has some bubbles. I wonder what will happen if she pours some in near the Falls?" yelled Peter.

"Look Emily has some bubbles. I wonder if she'll pour some in?" yelled PJ.

"It is REALLY loud. Look I have bubbles! What do you think will happen if I pour a bit in near the Falls?" asked Emily.

PJ started to imagine what it would be like if Emily did pour some of her bubbles into the Falls, and what if the bottle slipped and she poured in way too many bubbles.

Maybe it is not such a great idea. I might get lost in bubbles instead of lost under the Falls. I would be so small that the bubbles would lift me up. And then I might think OH MY. NOW WHAT? It would be the biggest bubble bath ever. And Emily would say, "OH NO! PJ's floating away on a cloud of bubbles! Oh no! How am I ever to get him back now? PJ! PJ!"

And then all his family would watch as he went higher, and higher up in the air on a cloud of bubbles. And then he would ask, "What was that?" as he turned to look back at his tail covered in bubbles saying "That tickles!" And then he would think, *Oh no, the bubbles are popping!*

Pop,

    pop,

        POP,

            pop,

    POP,

  pop,

POP,

    pop,

        POP,

      POP,

  pop,

    pop,

POP,

      pop,

  pop,

    POP,

    POP,

pop.

And he'd tumble back down toward the rushing water.

No, no, no. This wasn't a good plan at all. "I don't think you should put any bubbles in the Falls Emily," PJ told her. "I think it might make too many and carry me away. You know how I always get into scrapes. Although I would probably be very clean after such a big bubble bath."

"Funny little mouse. You do come up with the some interesting ideas sometimes!" Emily laughed, but she put her container of bubbles back in her pocket just to be safe.

Chapter Five

IN WHICH PJ EXPLORES QUEBEC CITY

PJ was quite confused. He had woken up that morning and stepped outside the fifth-wheel to do his daily stretching exercises—not that they seemed to help much; no matter how much he stretched, he never seemed to get any taller—

Now, what had he been thinking? Oh, right, how confused he was! He just did not seem to be able to understand anything people said anymore.

He had said "Hello" to someone walking by and they had said "Bon..."something back. He did not really know what and thought it was a very peculiar reply.

Then he had said "Hello. Isn't it a wonderful day to do one's stretching exercises?" to someone else and they had

said "Bon…" something, and then "Jenacompra," which was a word PJ had never heard before and had no idea what it meant. So he had given up trying to talk to people and had just concentrated on stretching until it was time for breakfast.

"Emily?"

"Yes, PJ?"

"Can you say something to me?"

"Like what?"

"Oh, I don't know. Anything at all really."

"Why?"

"Well, I seem to have lost my ability to understand and I just wanted to check it."

"Hmmm. Well, you seem to be able to understand me right now. Is what we're saying enough to be able to check your understanding do you think?"

"I'm not sure. I suppose it might be. It's just that when I went outside this morning to do my stretching exercises, and I said hello to people passing by, I didn't understand what they said back to me."

"I think they were probably speaking French because we are in Quebec now and they speak French here," Rebecca informed them helpfully.

"Oh. Yes, well, that would explain why I did not understand, since as far as I can remember, I don't think I know any French. Do I?" PJ asked Emily.

"I shouldn't think so. At least I've never taught you any. But it wouldn't hurt to learn a bit while we're here. Rebecca, can you help us learn some basic things to say? It might help PJ to be less confused."

"Sure!" Rebecca said. "I'll bring my French phrase book with me and we can learn some things along the way as we explore Old Quebec. Come on then let's find Peter and Megan and get going."

And so they set off to explore the old part of Quebec City. Compared to anything else they had seen so far in Canada it did seem very old. The houses were mostly made of brick or stone and were attached together instead of being set in their own yards. Many of the streets were made of cobblestones and the old city was surrounded by stone walls. It all seemed like it was from another age and not like the rest of Canada at all. Everything was so quaint and picturesque.

"I really like it here," said Emily. "I don't suppose we could stay could we?"

"I doubt it. It is the other side of the country from home and all our friends," Rebecca replied.

"Yes, that's true. But it is very nice!"

"What are these walls for? They're very tall and wide," said PJ.

"These are the Old Quebec ramparts. They're the only fortified city walls in North America north of Mexico. They were built around 1759 after the British took the city of Quebec from the French. The walls were built to protect the city, which was first settled in 1608."

"Why, why do we ask any questions when we know Rebecca will give us such exciting answers?" said Megan, in a please-spare-me-the-details tone of voice.

"Well, it's good to have some knowledge of where you're going, you know," Rebecca replied. "If PJ knew a bit of French he would not have felt so confused this morning when he was doing his stretching exercises."

"That is very true. Not only did I not understand anyone, but I also did a lot of stretching exercises and I am no taller than I was this morning. It is all so very disappointing really," PJ sighed.

"Funny little mouse," said Emily.

"So, how do you say 'hello' or 'good morning'?" PJ asked.

"Bonjour," replied Rebecca.

"That sounds exactly like what people said to me this morning! Is that how you say hello?"

"That's right. And to say your name you say 'Je m'appelle Rebecca,' except you would say 'PJ' of course. And to say 'thank you' you say 'merci.'"

"I like that! It sounds nice," said Emily.

"Wow, what is that?" asked Peter suddenly, pointing to a huge slope in the middle of everything.

"That's the ice slide. You can ride down it in the winter—when it's frozen—on a toboggan," Rebecca told him.

"Oh, I wish it were wintertime. That looks like sooooo much fun! Can we come back do you think? I would love to go down the slide," said PJ, imagining himself whizzing by.

"Probably
not this winter.
But it would be fun
sometime. I think you can
also skate on the river and they
have a big ice sculpture competi-
tion," said Rebecca.

"That ALL sounds like heaps of
fun! At least I will have time to learn
some more French before we come
back, and maybe how to ice skate as
well," said PJ, picturing himself in a
cute little pair of skates.

"Oui. C'est exact."

"What?"

"I said, 'yes, that's right,'" Rebecca told
him.

"Oh. I think I have a lot to learn!" said PJ.

"And just think of all the other countries in
the world we have yet to go to that we don't know
the languages of. There is just so much to know and
explore," Emily said.

"Oh dear. I don't think my stuffing can hold that much
information!"

"Well, we shall see how much we can cram in your
head over time," said Rebecca.

"Will that make the stuffing in my head any bigger do
you think?" PJ asked.

"No, I shouldn't think so."

"Oh fiddlesticks. Nothing ever seems to make me any bigger no matter what I do."

"I like you just the size you are," said Emily.

"Why thank you. I suppose I am about the right size for riding around on your shoulder."

"You funny little mouse. Come on, let's go back to the fifth-wheel. My legs are smaller than Rebecca's and I'm tired from walking everywhere."

"Your legs are nowhere near as small as mine," PJ reminded her.

"That's true. Your legs must feel almost completely worn off!"

"They are a bit tired," he admitted.

And so they returned to their home on wheels for a bit of a rest.

chapter six

IN WHICH PJ EXPLORES THE
OCEAN FLOOR

They traveled all through Quebec, where people said things like "Bonjour," and "Merci," and PJ himself learned to say things like "Je m'appelle PJ." Then they drove through New Brunswick and over one of the longest bridges in the world to a lovely place called Prince Edward Island, that had red earth, green and pink fields, and blue water. Now they were going to the Bay of Fundy in Nova Scotia, which had the highest tides in the whole world. PJ was not sure what was so interesting about high tides, but he supposed his family knew what they were doing. At least he hoped they did, although sometimes he was not so sure.

"Here we are," said Dad as they arrived.

They all piled out of the truck to see the very normal sight of an ocean bay.

"I don't know, Dad, this is nice with the steep red cliffs

and all, but what are we supposed to do here?" asked Peter.

"We're going to watch the tide go out."

"That sounds like heaps of fun," said Megan, rolling her eyes. "How incredibly exciting!"

"Megan, stop being so sarcastic. It might not be too bad to watch. This is the location of the highest tides in the whole world. I read that the water flow in and out of here in one tide cycle is more than the flow of all the freshwater rivers of the world put together. It's supposed to go up and down quite quickly once it gets going," stated Rebecca. "You don't want to get caught down in

the bay when the water starts to come in."

"Oh, well, that definitely makes it sound way, way more interesting," said Megan, in a humph-whatever tone of voice.

Does it? Hmmm, I respectfully disagree, thought PJ.

"Come on, let's go down. The water is almost gone and we can walk on the ocean floor. Come on Emily, let's see what we can find," said Rebecca.

They all set off in single file, climbing down the steep red cliffs of the bay to the ocean floor. The sea life left behind in the tidal pools was amazing. Rebecca picked up little wee crabs and showed them to Emily and PJ.

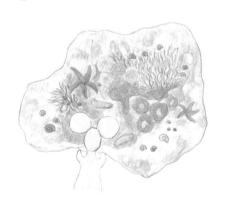

There were all sorts of colours of starfish, sea urchins, hermit crabs, and other things that they had never seen before.

"These creatures are even smaller than me!" PJ exclaimed.

"There are lots of things that are smaller than you PJ," said Rebecca.

"Are there? Well that is comforting to know."

"Funny little mouse."

Rebecca, looking up at the surrounding cliffs, noticed that the water was starting to come back in.

"Look the tide is coming back in. And fast. Wow!

Come on, we better start heading back up the cliffs."

Emily, reaching up to hang onto PJ, who had been perched on her shoulder, suddenly exclaimed, "Rebecca, I can't find PJ! He was just on my shoulder and now he is NOT!"

"He must have fallen off into the water. We can't really stop to look now; the tide is coming in too fast."

Meanwhile PJ was bobbing along on the crest of a wave, which was moving very quickly towards the cliff face. *Oh dear, dear me and oh no,* he thought. *What have I got myself into now? I always seem to be getting into trouble.*

As the water reached the cliff face it started to move upwards at a great rate, swirling and churning, and churning and swirling. *This is like being on a merry-go-round of water. Oh my goodness gracious me, I really do hope I don't end up slamming into the cliff face!* thought PJ as he once again found himself hurtling towards the cliffs. Then he found himself spun round and heading out to sea as the wave receded. *Oh bother, now what? I really, really don't want to end up out at sea all that much either.* "OH, HELP!" he called. "OH PLEASE SOMEONE, HELP!"

But there was not a single person to be found who could rescue PJ as he rushed up and up

and up,

and up

the cliff face,

and round

and round

and round

on the incoming tide.

"SQUAK, SQUUAAAK."

"OH. Oh, my word! You scared me almost to death, and I am already plenty scared enough, if you don't mind," PJ said to the seagull that suddenly appeared above him.

"Eh, what's that you thay thonny?" said the seagull with a very pronounced lisp. "Thcared? Ain't no reathon to be thcared. Just a thpot of fun, eh. Don't mind, no I don't mind. Came to join you for the ride. Don't mind if I do. Quite the thpot of fun wouldn't you thay. Eh? I take thith ride every day. You thould too. Do you a world of good. But I must thay you do look ath timid ath a mouthe."

"I *am* a mouse."

"Ah ha! You don't thay. Well that explainth it then, eh."

"Explains what?"

"Why your being timid of courthe. Eh, I thay, are you really thcared and not enjoying yourthelf?"

"Not overly much in all honesty," PJ admitted.

"Well, well. I am thorry to hear that. I could give you a lift to thore if you like. Eh, what do you thay to that then?"

"I would be most obliged I am sure, and my Emily would probably be happy to see me. She must be a bit worried by now."

"You have an Emily do you, eh. And what exactly might an Emily be?"

"She is a very cute, nice little girl that looks after me."

"Ah well, we can't be worrying cute, nithe little girlth, eh, even for the thake of a fun ride in the thea. Come on

then, I'll give you a lift," and with that the seagull picked PJ up by his tail.

As the seagull flew by his friends he declared…

"Guysth, guysth, I found a mouthe. And heth all fat, and cute and thtripey!" and with that the seagull opened his mouth and PJ was delivered right back to Emily.

"Thank you ever so much for rescuing me," PJ said. "I am very grateful. I am sorry for disturbing your ride though."

"Not to worry. I can ride the wave up again tomorrow, and every day after that. Look after your Emily now. I must thay, she does look extremely happy to thee you, eh."

"Bye, bye!" called PJ as he waved to the seagull and flopped his soggy self down next to Emily.

"I must say, PJ, you do get into some interesting situations, but then you always seem to come out of them with the help of your friends," said Rebecca.

"It *was* rather an eventful day. And just when I thought the day was going to be boring. I mean really, the thought of watching the tide go in and out did not sound overly inspiring."

"You certainly managed to liven up our last day

travelling across Canada," said Megan.

"Is this our last day here? Where are we going tomorrow?"

"Tomorrow we head home," said Rebecca, "but I am sure you will find plenty of adventures along the way."

"I have a feeling you might be right, but that is too bad. I like travelling," said PJ.

"Me too. But it'll be nice to see our friends and Nanny and the cat again."

"A CAT! You have a cat? Mice don't usually like cats too much as they seem to like us quite a lot, mostly as lunch!" PJ said worriedly.

chapter seven

IN WHICH PJ IS AMAZED BY FLOWERS AND FIREWORKS

The whole family arrived back home in Victoria, B.C.. They had driven across Canada, all the way from the Bay of Fundy in Nova Scotia.

"It is nice to stay still for a change, isn't it PJ?" Emily asked him.

"I guess so," said PJ in a not-really, and I-don't-think-so kind of voice. "But I must admit, that I did like seeing all the new and interesting places and meeting different people. Things seem a bit dull now."

"Well, cheer up PJ. Tonight we are going to finish off our big trip by going to

Butchart Gardens to see all the pretty flowers and then a fireworks show. And, we are taking a picnic dinner," said Emily.

"That does sound nice. I quite like flowers, fireworks, and picnics. Do you think there might be some cheese at the picnic? I am quite partial to cheese."

"I would think there will be a bit of cheese for you. So you see how much you have to look forward to today. And tomorrows excitement is that we get our cat back from Nanny's house!"

"Hmmm. I'm not sure if that sounds so nice or not. I'm a bit scared of cats. I've heard they usually like to chase little mouses such as myself."

"Yes, but our cat is not likely to chase you because you are a special mouse, a cute, stuffed PJ-type mouse. And besides, our cat is way too lazy to bother chasing anything. So, I wouldn't worry too much." Emily tried to reassure PJ.

"Well, if you say so Emily. But I still think I would feel safer if you had some other kind of pet that maybe didn't like to chase little mouses…say, a goldfish or maybe a hummingbird."

"A hummingbird! Why a hummingbird?"

"Well, mostly because they are so

small that I don't think it could carry me off like most other birds could," PJ told her.

"Yes. I suppose you have a point. But we don't have a hummingbird, or a goldfish. We only have a very lazy cat. Maybe you could chase him and stop him from being so lethargic." Emily suggested.

"No, no, that is quite unnecessary. I think I will much prefer him being le...le... leth...hmmm, what you said," PJ replied.

"Anyway, come on PJ, it's time to go now," said Emily, and they set off to join the rest of the family.

Fortunately the drive to Butchart Gardens was very short. PJ was quite happy about this as he was just a little tired of being in the truck. It had been a very, very long drive back across Canada.

"Rebecca, how long will it take to look at the flowers before we get to have our picnic?" asked Peter, who was not all that interested in flowers. "I'm getting hungry."

"Well, it usually takes about two hours to walk around the gardens. Apparently they have nine hundred varieties of flowers in the summer in all sorts of colours. What is even more amazing is that they plant three hundred thousand bulbs for the springtime and for Christmas they put up so many Christmas lights that they don't even know how many they have. But on one tree alone there are two thousand, eight hundred," said Rebecca informatively.

"I knew I shouldn't have asked you a question. I just wanted to know how long 'til food," muttered Peter.

"You know, I think that maybe you are turning into a walking Wikipedia," Megan said to Rebecca.

"I know! It's all so interesting and there is so much more I can tell you," her sister replied.

"No, no, no. Just let me look and….."

Megan stopped in awe as they all gazed down at the Sunken Garden.

"Wow!"

"That's sooooo nice," said Peter, thinking that maybe flowers were not so bad after all.

"Look at all the different colours and shapes. It's like Niagara Falls but in flowers," said Megan. "All the way across Canada and back and I never saw anything as colourful as this. And right in our own backyard too."

"This is your back yard?" asked PJ in amazement.

"No, no. That's just an expression for something that's close to home."

"Oh," said PJ in disappointment. "I would have quite liked this as a back yard."

"It is pretty spectacular, and there is still so much more to see. There's the Rose Garden and the Italian Garden and the Japanese Garden," Rebecca replied knowingly.

And so they wandered around all of the gardens, amazed at the vast array of beauty until they did start to get very hungry.

"This is all very well, but when do we get to have our picnic? I really am hungry," said Peter.

"Come on then. I think the fireworks start soon, so we should get back to the picnic area."

Back at the picnic area Mom and Dad had all the food laid out. PJ found a small piece of cheese that was just the right size for him, and started to nibble contentedly. As the rest of the family started to tuck into their picnic, the first of the fireworks began.

The fireworks were as amazing as the flowers had been. There were the normal kind that went up in the air in all sorts of colours, accompanied by loud *POP, BOOM,*

BANGS, but what was really neat were the ones down low over the lake, all choreographed and set to music. They were made to look like serpents going through the water, and fish jumping up a waterfall, and bees buzzing around a hive, and ladies dancing, and elephants walking away into the distance. PJ had had no idea that fireworks could be made into so many different moving scenes. He had never seen anything like it before.

For once PJ was almost speechless. *Hmmm, maybe being home would not be so dull after all,* he thought. And he did have the meeting of the cat to look forward to as well, although he still had his doubts about how fun that might be for a small mouse such as himself.

chapter Eight

IN WHICH PJ MEETS THE CAT

They were home and it was a day like many others. PJ was resting on Emily's bed. He was thinking happy thoughts, reminiscing about the places he had been and the characters he had met.

He was humming to himself "hmmmm, hmmm, hmmm" in a drowsy sort of way when he was startled out of his reverie by the shaking of the bed.

Oh my goodness. What was that? thought PJ in fright as his eyes snapped open.

There before him was an enormous, white, fuzzy creature.

"MEOW!" said the mass of white fur.

"Oh, hello. I say, I really don't think you should jump on beds and startle very small mouses that way."

"Sorry," the creature said, "but it looked a good place for a cat nap."

"Yes, well, it is a wonderful place for a mouse nap so it just might suit a cat too. But then I don't know, not being a cat myself."

"I suppose if I join you then I could let you know if it is a good spot for a cat or not, since I am in fact a cat," said the cat as he plonked himself down…and everything suddenly went dark for PJ.

"I say, I hmmm hmmm hmmmm. Phsst hmm hhhmmm."

"Pardon?" replied the cat as he shifted himself into his favourite position, which was on his back with all four paws in the air.

"I said, I say, I do believe you have plonked yourself on my head. Would you mind moving just a tad? You are frightfully heavy."

"Well, if you insist. But really I was quite comfy. You make just the right sort of pillow for a cat."

"Well, I do think it would be most polite, if you are going to use me as a pillow, that you might at least introduce yourself properly," PJ suggested.

"Ah, yes, well, that is rather difficult."

"How so? How can it be difficult to introduce oneself?"

"Well, I have many names but not one in particular you see,"

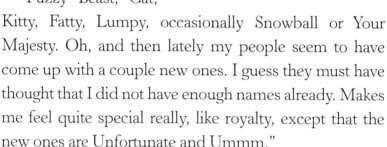

the cat told him.

"Oh. I see," said PJ, not really seeing at all. "All the same, what are you called?"

"Fuzzy Beast, Cat, Kitty, Fatty, Lumpy, occasionally Snowball or Your Majesty. Oh, and then lately my people seem to have come up with a couple new ones. I guess they must have thought that I did not have enough names already. Makes me feel quite special really, like royalty, except that the new ones are Unfortunate and Ummm."

"What is unfortunate, and ummmm what?"

Those are my new names, Unfortunate and Ummm. But mostly they just call me Fuzzy."

"Well, Ummm, that does seem most unfortunate. But Fuzzy seems quite appropriate," said PJ with a sneeze as the cat hair was tickling his nose. "Still, as PJ your pillow talking, I would be most grateful if you would find a different sort of pillow. You see, I am quite small for a mouse and it is kind of dark and stuffy under here, and I am feeling quite, quite squished," declared PJ as he tried to wiggle himself free. *Hmmmm, maybe Fatty and Lumpy don't seem so inappropriate*

either, thought PJ.

"If you're going to wriggle like that I won't get any sleep at all. You realize, of course, that you are disturbing my mandatory eighteen hours of cat napping."

"Hmm hmm hmmm hmm hmmm hmmm hmmm hm," PJ muttered.

"I beg your pardon? I did not quite catch that," the cat replied.

"I said, eighteen hours, is that per day? That seems a bit extreme."

"But of course. I am a cat after all and I have my repu-tation to maintain."

"What is a repu...repu...hmm, what you said?"

"A reputation. It's what you are known for."

"So sleeping eighteen hours a day, what kind of re-pu-ta-tion does that maintain?"

"Why one of cuteness of course!" the cat said with delight.

"I think you lost me."

"Well, I have a vast array of different sleeping positions, each one I have perfected to be extremely endearing. It keeps the family highly entertained."

"Oh. And what do you do with the other... ummm," PJ stopped to count on his fingers, gave up in despair, and ended with, "hmmm, umm, the rest of the hours of the day?"

"Well, I do find it quite fun to chase mice in the park."

"Oh," said PJ thinking that he did not like the sound of that and maybe he did not mind being a pillow so much after all.

The End...

(until the next adventure!)

ATHABASCA GLACIER

LAKE MANITOU

BUTCHART GARDENS

PJ's

Canadian adventure!

QUEBEC
CITY

BAY OF
FUNDY

NIAGARA
FALLS

THE FURTHER TRAVEL
ADVENTURES OF PJ MOUSE

*Coming in early 2014 is the second
book in the series:*

The Travel
Adventures of PJ Mouse

• in Queensland, Australia •

As The Travel Adventures of PJ Mouse continues, PJ
finds himself in the land downunder, exploring the tropi-
cal state of Queensland. Come discover new places, and
friends, as PJ snorkels at the Great Barrier Reef, con-
verses with a Loggerhead turtle in the midst of a great

undertaking, and takes a flight over the rainforest on the back of a lorikeet. Finally, upon returning home, PJ finds that Fuzzy Beast has found himself a new pillow......

Also, coming soon are, The Travel Adventures of PJ Mouse, in New Zealand and The Travel Adventures of PJ Mouse, in a small corner of England. As well, PJ Mouse, the stuffed animal character, will be available along with his own passport and stickers to track his trips.

For more information on PJ Mouse and where to find him on his next adventure, check out my author webpage at **www.PJMouse.com** *and be sure to Like him on Facebook at* **www.facebook.com/GwynethJanePage**

ABOUT THE ILLUSTRATOR

Megan Elizabeth, Jane's second oldest daughter, has lived in Australia and Canada, and has travelled extensively with her family — and PJ! Having been artistic since she was a little girl, illustrating this book has enabled her to combine her love of travel with her love of art. She currently resides in Victoria, Canada and is attending the Western Academy of Photography to further her skills as a professional photographer.

ABOUT THE AUTHOR

Gwyneth Jane Page, who holds an MBA from Simon Fraser University, has called many countries home. She grew up in such places as Peru, the United States, England, the Caribbean, and now resides in Victoria, Canada with her husband and four children. The Travel Adventures of PJ Mouse series is based on the Page family's journey with the real stuffed animal, PJ, who was found by Jane's youngest daughter, Emily.

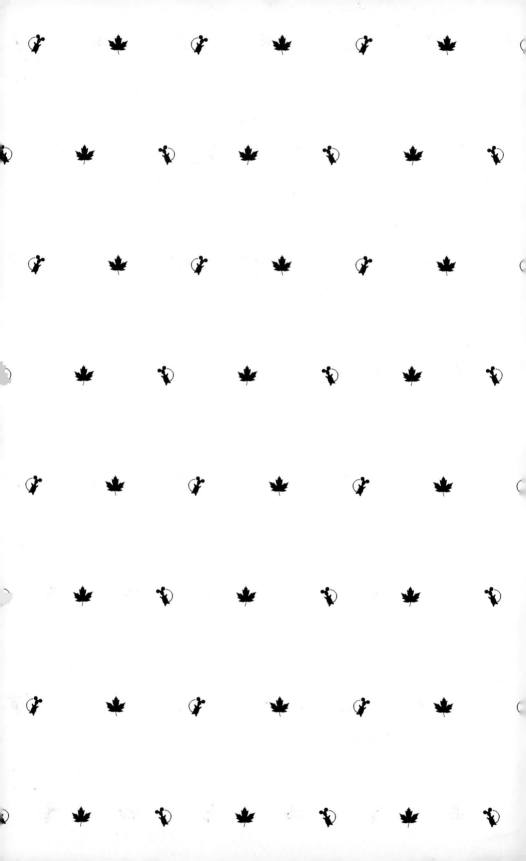

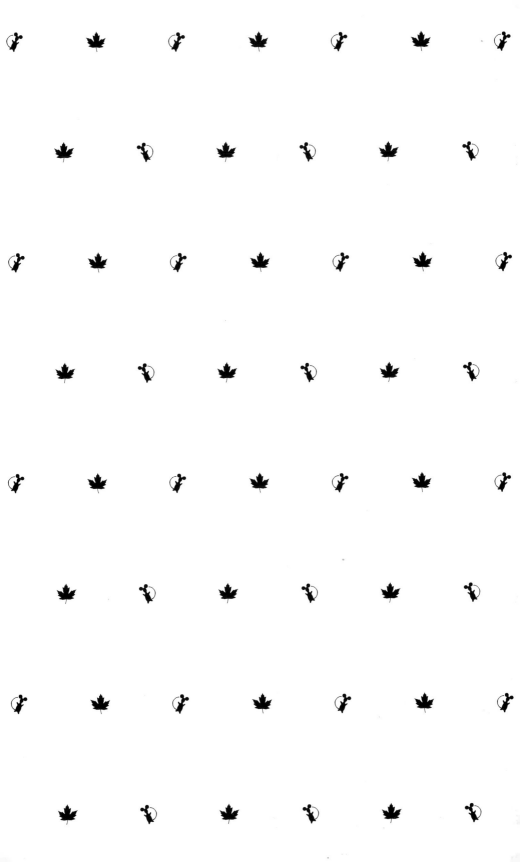

Printed in Canada